A Little Witch Magic

To Christina, who has cast her own magic spell on me

A Little Witch Magic

by Robert Bender

Henry Holt and Company ★ New York

Broomhelga had a reputation as the meanest witch in town. Everyone was afraid to walk down her street. Everyone, that is, except for one little girl named Wanda. Secretly, *she* was curious.

Some folks in town said they'd seen Broomhelga swooping down on her broom, chasing terrified dogs back into their doghouses and scaring the birds out of trees. Others didn't believe it. But everyone agreed that when smoke billowed out of her chimney, Broomhelga was up to no good.

Wanda couldn't understand what the fuss was about. She thought it all seemed rather exciting.

As for Broomhelga, she thought her life was quite routine. She'd have her usual lizard-seaweed stew for breakfast, then feed all the spiders that had decorated her home with beautiful webs.

She spent most days hunched over her garden, pulling out thick gnarled roots, toadstools, and evil-smelling weeds to use as ingredients in her magic potions.

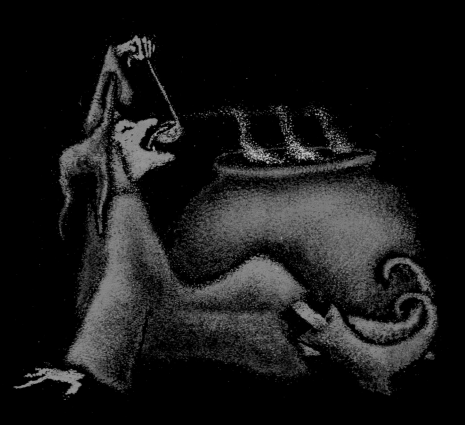

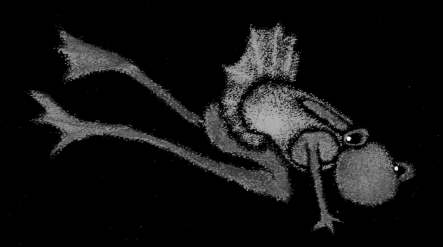

Broomhelga tested her potions and spells on the frogs in her backyard pond. She would have preferred to test them on real live human beings — but none ever dared to stop by. (Wanda wanted to, but even *she* was afraid to visit the witch alone.)

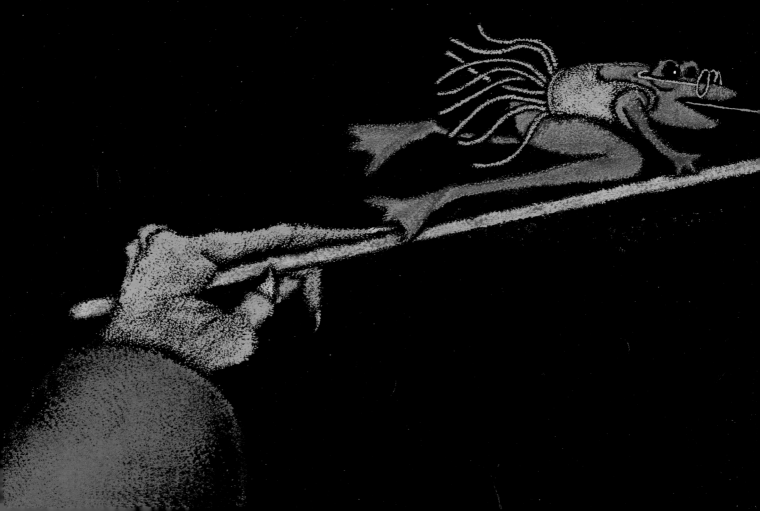

Poor Broomhelga! She thought it wasn't fair that no one ever came to visit her. After all, she wasn't trying to be mean. She was just doing what witches do.

But with only the frogs and her black cat for
company, Broomhelga had become lonely and bored.
Even her daily broomstick tours weren't fun anymore.

Luckily, Halloween was coming soon. Broomhelga couldn't wait! She spent a whole week making naughty plans and mixing powerful potions.
Halloween was her favorite night of the year!

It was the children's favorite night too. They were all excited
about their costumes — but Wanda was especially thrilled. She
couldn't wait to wear the big pointy hat that topped off her
witch's costume. Maybe this year she could even convince her
friends to go to Broomhelga's house.

After supper the children ran through the neighborhood, yelling
"Trick or treat!" and collecting lots of candy.

Finally they reached the deserted street where Broomhelga lived.
   "I dare you to go to the witch's house!" cried a little ghost.
   "There's no such thing as a real witch," insisted a little mummy.
"Is there?"
   "Sure there is," said Wanda. "But I'm not afraid. I'm a witch too!"
With that, she marched down the street, dragging her broom. The
others followed hesitantly.

Broomhelga peeked out the window. She couldn't believe her good luck. Lots of juicy children had delivered themselves right to her doorstep! She rubbed her hands together with glee. "What spell shall I use first?" she wondered.

Cautiously the children climbed the rickety porch s
"What cool Halloween decorations!" said Wanda.
She banged on the door.

The door creaked open. With a cackle, Broomhelga appeared in the doorway. The children were so stunned that they forgot to say "Trick or treat."

Even Wanda couldn't believe what she saw. So this
was what the witch looked like up close!

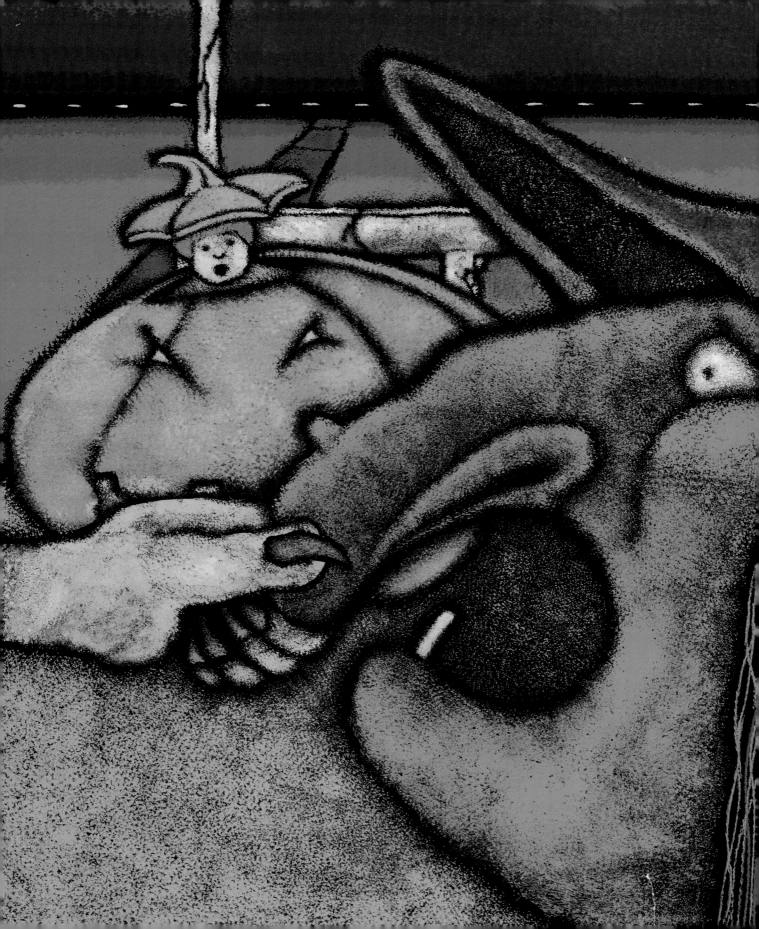

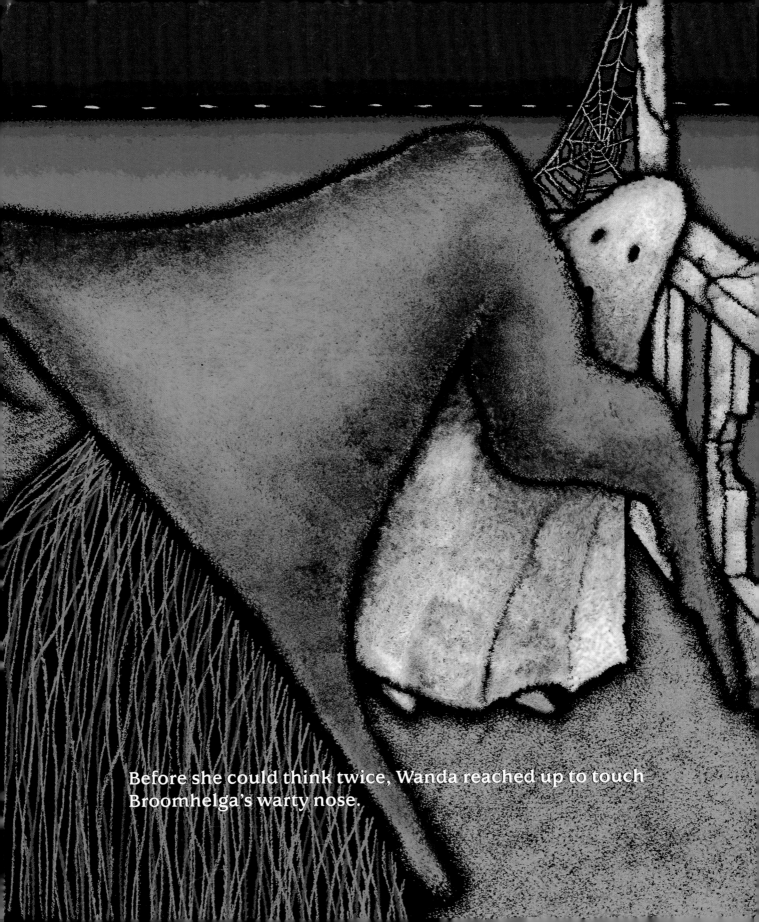

Before she could think twice, Wanda reached up to touch Broomhelga's warty nose.

That was a mistake! Broomhelga let out a horrible shriek.
All the children ran in terror, except Wanda.

She was delighted.
She'd met the witch at last!

"Are you a good witch or a bad witch?" Wanda asked.
Broomhelga scratched her head. "I don't know.
I never thought about that before. I guess I'm a —"
But before she could finish her sentence, Wanda
did what she had so often dreamed. She jumped on

Broomhelga's broomstick. "Take me for a ride," she
begged. "Pretty please?"
     Broomhelga decided to oblige her. It might be
thrilling to have a passenger screaming for mercy.

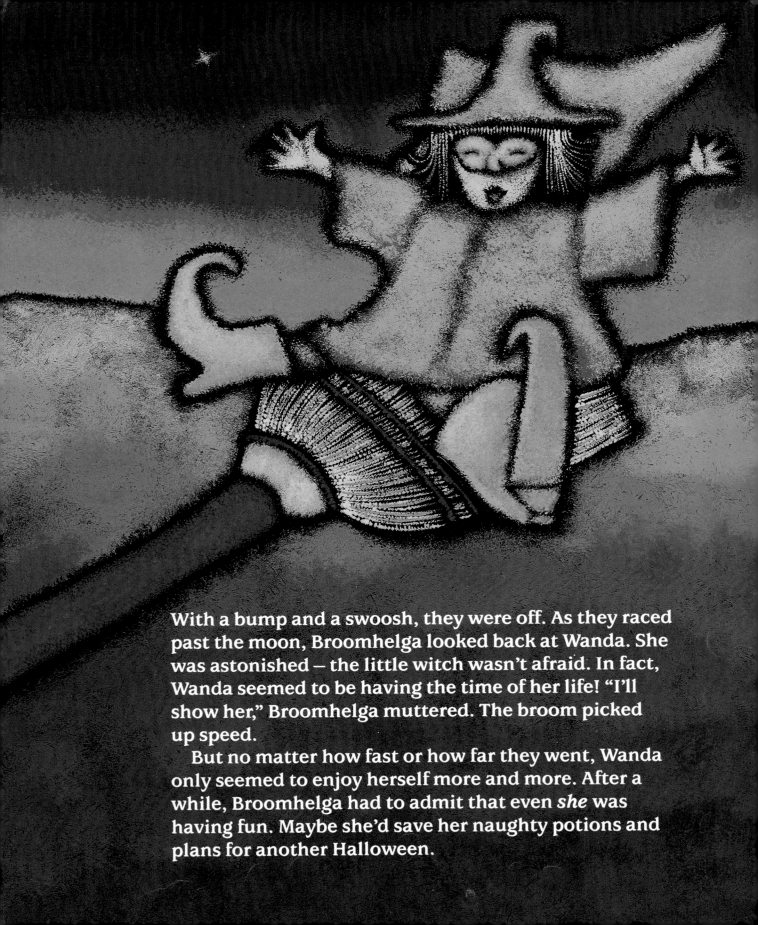

With a bump and a swoosh, they were off. As they raced past the moon, Broomhelga looked back at Wanda. She was astonished — the little witch wasn't afraid. In fact, Wanda seemed to be having the time of her life! "I'll show her," Broomhelga muttered. The broom picked up speed.

But no matter how fast or how far they went, Wanda only seemed to enjoy herself more and more. After a while, Broomhelga had to admit that even *she* was having fun. Maybe she'd save her naughty potions and plans for another Halloween.

They tore past the Big Dipper, sped through the galaxy, and finally flew back toward the moon. Wanda yawned. It was past her bedtime, but she was having too much fun to go home just yet. "Broomhelga!" she shouted happily. "I think you're a good witch, a *very* good witch indeed! Let's do this again soon!"

"We'll see," grumbled Broomhelga. But secretly, she had a feeling this first ride wouldn't be their last.

Copyright © 1992 by Robert Bender
All rights reserved, including the right to reproduce
this book or portions thereof in any form.
First edition
Published by Henry Holt and Company, Inc.,
115 West 18th Street, New York, New York 10011.
Published simultaneously in Canada
by Fitzhenry & Whiteside Limited,
91 Granton Drive, Richmond Hill, Ontario L4B 2N5.

Library of Congress Cataloging-in-Publication Data
Bender, Robert.
 A little witch magic / by Robert Bender.
 Summary: A lonely witch never has any visitors
until one Halloween when a young girl, who is
more fascinated than frightened, comes to call.
 ISBN 0-8050-2126-4
 [1. Witches – Fiction.   2. Halloween – Fiction.]
I. Title.   PZ. B43147Li   1992   [E] – dc20   92-4054

Printed in the United States of America
on acid-free paper. ∞

10 9 8 7 6 5 4 3 2 1

Designed by Robert Olsson